But Who Will Bell the Cats?

Long ago, the mice had a general council to consider what measures they could take to outwit their common enemy, the Cat. Some said this, and some said that; but at last a young mouse got up and said he had a proposal to make, which he thought would meet the case. "You will all agree," said he, "that our chief danger consists in the sly and treacherous manner in which the enemy approaches us. Now, if we could receive some signal of her approach, we could easily escape from her. I venture, therefore, to propose that a small bell be procured, and attached by a ribbon round the neck of the Cat. By this means we should always know when she was about, and could easily retire while she was in the neighborhood." This proposal met with general applause, until an old mouse got up and said, "That is all very well, but who is to bell the Cat?"

—Aesop's Fables

For
Claire Beaulieu
ma petite cherie and *godchild.*

Thank you to my talented family for their help and *support, especially*
Louis Carrozza, *royal architect;* **Frances Carrozza**, *royal seamstress;*
Veronica Carrozza O'Dell, *royal chef;* **Russell Farhang**, *royal advisor;*
Brian Azer, *my book designer* & *website designer;*
Houghton Mifflin: the editor **Kate O'Sullivan**,
the creative director **Sheila Smallwood**, *and the publicist* **Jennifer Taber;**
Fran Diesu *from the Tee Ridder Miniatures Museum at the*

Nassau County Museum of Art
and **Diane Matyas** *from the Staten Island Museum.*

COPYRIGHT © 2009 BY CYNTHIA VON BUHLER

WWW.HMHBOOKS.COM

ALL RIGHTS RESERVED. FOR INFORMATION ABOUT
PERMISSION TO REPRODUCE SELECTIONS FROM THIS
BOOK, WRITE TO PERMISSIONS, HOUGHTON MIFFLIN
HARCOURT PUBLISHING COMPANY, 215 PARK AVENUE
SOUTH, NEW YORK, NEW YORK 10003.

HOUGHTON MIFFLIN BOOKS FOR CHILDREN IS
AN IMPRINT OF HOUGHTON MIFFLIN HARCOURT
PUBLISHING COMPANY.

The text of this book is set in Salmiak and First Grade.

Library of Congress Cataloging-in-Publication Data

Buhler, Cynthia von.
But who will bell the cats? / by Cynthia von Buhler.
p. cm.
Summary: While a princess spoils her eight cats, a mouse and his friend, a brown bat, live on scraps in the castle cellar, but Mouse decides to
place bells on the cats' necks so that he and Brown Bat might live comfortably as well. Includes the Aesop fable on which the story is based.
ISBN 978-0-618-99718-3
[1. Mice–Fiction. 2. Bats–Fiction. 3. Cats–Fiction. 4. Princesses–Fiction.] I. Title.
PZ7.B911135But 2009
[E]–dc22
2008050165

But Who Will Bell the Cats?

By Cynthia von Buhler

Houghton Mifflin Books for Children

Houghton Mifflin Harcourt
Boston   New York   2009

In a castle high upon a hill there lived a princess and her eight cats. The princess doted on her cats. She did not want them to catch colds or to dirty their fur, so they were not allowed to go outside or down into the drafty cellar.

Down in the drafty cellar lived a mouse and his only friend, a brown bat.

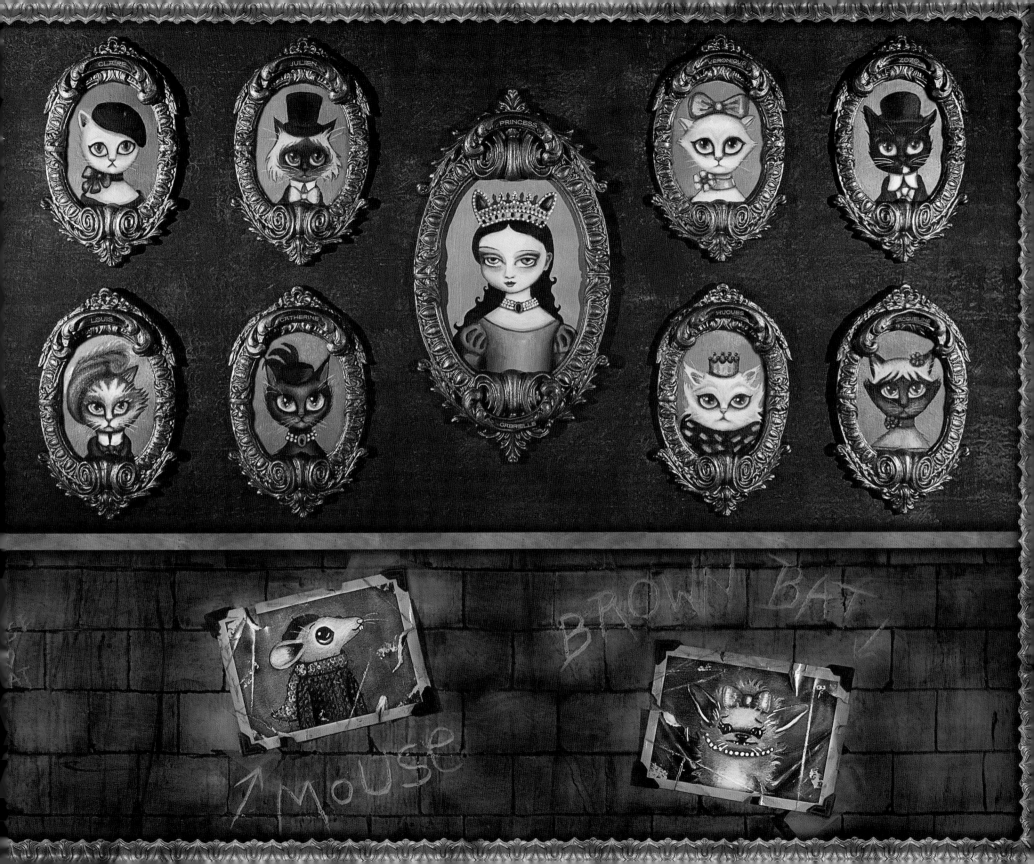

Upstairs, the cats ate at the banquet table in the elegant dining hall.

Down below, Mouse ate crumbs that fell through the floorboards into the basement.

Upstairs, the cats slept in soft beds with perfumed pillows.

Down below, Mouse slept in a matchbox covered with an old, smelly sock.

One night, Mouse said to his friend, "I will make myself armor and a sword so I can travel upstairs and place bells around the cats' necks. If we bell the cats, we will always be warned by the jingling sound when they are nearby. Then we, too, can sleep on perfumed pillows."

"What is wrong with the sock? It's soft," said Brown Bat.

Mouse worked for weeks on his armor. When it was complete the two friends headed upstairs with ribbon and a sack of bells. They got as far as the game room when they were spotted.

Mouse poked at the cats with his little sword, but that only got them excited. The cats had a fabulous time playing Mouse Ping-Pong that day until Brown Bat distracted them with a song and dance.

Humiliated, Mouse escaped through a hole under the stairs.

Autumn passed, and the cats
read by the fireplace in the
wood-paneled library.

Mouse read newspaper scraps
in the dark, dingy den.

Winter came, and the cats took bubble baths in the powder room.

Mouse bathed under a pipe that dripped rusty water into his chilly chamber.

On a cold night Mouse said to Brown Bat, "Those cats are not afraid of a small mouse. I will make a dog costume to frighten them. We'll bell the scaredy-cats and then we, too, can take hot baths."

"Sounds dangerous!" said Brown Bat, frowning.

Mouse worked for weeks on the dog costume. When it was complete he and Brown Bat went upstairs with the collars hidden inside. They got as far as the front hall when they were spotted.

The cats were excited to see the entertaining mouse and bat in a dog costume. They had a wonderful time that night playing Mouse Floor Hockey until Brown Bat distracted the cats by dive-bombing them.

Humiliated, Mouse escaped through a hole under the kitchen sink.

Spring bloomed, and the cats held dances in the grand ballroom.

Mouse gathered trinkets that fell through the cracks of the floor into the damp basement.

Summer arrived, and on a hot, humid night Mouse said to Brown Bat, "I am smarter than those spoiled cats. We will present them a fashion show to convince them that belled collars are the latest style from Paris. Then we, too, can dance in the ballroom. You can be my model."

"I'm not tall enough to be a model!" exclaimed Brown Bat.

Mouse worked for weeks on his fashion show. Finally, he and Brown Bat took the jeweled collars he had made from the trinkets that had fallen through the floor cracks and went upstairs. They got as far as the kitchen before they were spotted.

The cats watched the fashion show with great interest. They were concerned about being fashionable, but they were more interested in the little mouse and bat.

They had a fun-filled day preparing delicious bat and mouse pies that they could eat at the princess's upcoming birthday party.

Luckily, the princess arrived in the kitchen for her afternoon tea so Mouse and Brown Bat were rescued before the pies were baked. She washed them off and apologized for the cats' lack of manners.

Then the princess bid them adieu
with a fruit and cheese basket
and kissed them each on the nose.

Mouse, inspired by the princess's kindness, came up with a plan to bell the cats once and for all. He slept very well that night.

On the morning of the princess's birthday, Mouse wrapped his gift in old wallpaper and left it outside the castle door.

"Tonight we will go upstairs for the princess's birthday party!" cried Mouse.

"But who will bell the cats?" asked Brown Bat.

"The princess!" said Mouse.

And she did.